THE ART

OF

WORDS

Brittny D. Morehead

AUTHOR, PUBLISHER, GHOSTWRITER, POET

The Art of Words

Copyright © 2022 by Brittiny D. Morehead

Printed in the United States of America

First Printing, 2022

ISBN-13: 978-1-7357901-4-5

eBook ISBN-13: 978-1-7357901-7-6

Images of Brittiny D. Morehead by William Washington/Extreme Works Studio

Published by Eat My Lyrics Publishing Company, LLC

https://brittinydmorehead.com/publisher

DEDICATIONS

This book is dedicated to young

writers, new writers, old writers,

blue writers.

Let's continue to embody our

personalities and gifts through the

artistry of words- our creations from

within.

-Brittiny D. Morehead

TABLE OF CONTENTS

<u>HEY YOU</u>

Writing is my first love, and it's a love in which will never diminish because it continuously saves me from myself.

I have a savage obsession with the artistry of words, and everything they encompass. I presume to be a New York Times Best-Selling Author, one day.

Words are powerful; they can lift someone up or completely tear them down. Words can influence what we do; they can make us cry, kill ourselves, beat someone to a bloody pulp, love, hate, cry again, care, not care, and the list goes on.

Words can make us who we become.

Words can make us happy. They can make us sad. They can inspire us to BE amazing people who DO amazing things.

WORDS... are the true underdog in art today, but for some reason, people have forgotten that, so- I am here to remind them.

INTRODUCTION

The Art of Words is a place where your mind is allowed to roam freely. Here, we do not judge, and we do not place limits on creativity.

I drew to the words on each page as if they were my only hope for redemption. In everything that I write, I expose pieces of myself. Sometimes, it happens naturally and other times, I'm aiming to simply entertain my fans, or forgive myself for something in which occurred in my past life. I have dreamt about stories in which I felt the Lord was asking me to tell, but all too often, I write about different forms of who I am.

My influences for this collection derive from truth, curiosity, and pain. I was inspired to write each story for their own separate reasons, but they all reveal the same beautiful concept; I have a desire of ether burning in the depths of my core for words, and the amazing things that I can do with them.

This desire makes me want to climb mountains, act on impulse, be vulnerable, be free.

This book of short stories emerged from a portfolio I crafted in a Creative Writing course that I attended at a Community College; it's now in development to become much more- I figured a sneak peek was only fair.

My goal here is to inspire new writers and share with you all the beginnings of very many novels to come.

SYNOPSOS OF EA, STORY

<u>Hopeless</u>

This story is about loving someone that you can never truly belong to; it's about emptiness.

Chloe carries a great deal of emotion for a ghost in which loves her. This story showcases the reality of loneliness for a lot of successful women.

Men encounter loneliness as well, but they often find random women to fill such voids.

Women who are career-driven often fall for married men, ideas of men, or the lowest standards of who they would've possibly wanted.

This role/character is depicted in so many movies- I decided to take it but alter its typical storyline.

<u>Where there is Robbery, there is Love</u>

So, there's Kevin. He's a good guy for the most part, but life happened to him. After he suffered the cards in which had been dealt, he began to kill women and rob them for the nice things his mother never gave him.

Kevin ran into a woman that made him realize that he can steal everything in the world, but he could never steal love, he could never steal happiness.

She relayed this message out of fear, but she was desperate enough and intrigued enough to explore him

in the end.

<u>My Name is Kim</u>

This particular story is personal, as it gives insight on the very many battles I encountered when my mother passed away.

Grief can bring about many things. I channeled my anger into the pages, so that I could cope with losing her.

This story was written because I couldn't- nor did I want to, let her go. I became reckless and volatile because I wanted my mother back.

In the heap of it all, I desired to hurt people around me. I needed a way to do that without really "doing that," so instead of literally losing my mind in real life, I remembered that I could write the pain away... clear my chest, and get revenge, all at once.

My name is Kim is a horror story for the best of us. It's going to showcase the journey of a broken daughter who's tired of being broken. Brittiny and Kim will reunite, and when they do, there's going to be trouble.

The full version will be launched soon, and I'll be working with my dream producer to bring it to the big screen.

<u>She Had a Dream</u>

Entertainers have done a great job with providing us an image of what it means to be cocky. In some of the worst cases, death has become the product of such an ego.

We'd like to think that some would just understand, it's all fun and games, but for a lot of people- they don't live in this fantasy world in which has been created to entertain us. They live in real life, the parts that matter.

Well, Melanie most certainly had a dream. She longed for true love and real fame- which is great, but have her performances gotten to her head?

Will she ever to grind on another fan again?

<u>Bruises of a Lover's Fist</u>

This novel has been in the making since I was 17 years old. I never even knew what I was writing, I just began to create these sarcastic sentences on paper to distract myself with my boyfriend's abnormal obsession with sex.

He'd truly be fighting mad if I didn't have sex with him. I wanted to be busy, not laid up being plowed like a yard all day.

As a result, he'd come in late, past any decent hour in which he'd like for me to come. I, of course, gathered that he was cheating. My mind fed me a couple of lines at a time. Years later, I saw the potential and chose to add onto it.

This story is utilized to explore the minds of men and women with infidelities and secrets. I wanted to capture the most horrific relationship and allow the woman her grand opportunity to finally obtain revenge.

Brandi deals with Sebastian's foul play until it kills her, literally. Her ghost ends up haunting him and all the women that knew he was married.

Sebastian is forced to learn a lesson, where-to-as, most men never do; they continue to treat women badly.

I will also be working with my dream producer to bring this thriller to life, stay tuned.

HOPELESS

There lived a woman in a beautiful house; no kids, no husband- for he had left, and no youth.

She lived a wonderful life with the fame in which she had acquired for herself, but she was still missing true love.

Dressed up in fantasies of who she imagined herself to be, she never foresaw this emptiness.

"Chloe, are you there?"

She heard what felt like vibrations of a voice come over her.

"Chloe, are you there."

"Who goes there?" She says in a panic.

"I was sent to be by your side tonight... to keep you warm, to provide you company."

"Well, I NEVER! You show yourself this instant."

"I wouldn't say that if I were you... Chloe, I can't-?"

"Show yourself!!!" Chloe sat upward in her California King Bed, back firm and shoulders straight, as she prepared herself for the intruder.

"How did you get into my house? Where are you?"

A gust of what felt like wind blew across her chest like a breeze on the hottest day in hell.

Chloe stood up and slowly walked toward her bedroom door, ignited with the fear of someone knocking her out or killing her.

She stopped mid-way and turned around to face the presence behind her. As she stood there in fear, she felt another gust of wind caress her back and move up her spine. She quickly turned around and her arms went flailing in the air at anything that could possibly be there.

"I am here Chloe." He says grazing her hair and touching her back once more.

At this point, Chloe was in tears. A spark of energy came over her as she sprinted away from her room and toward the front door of her luxury home. Did I fail to mention that it was all glass? Completely modeled for the diva that she was and tailored to fit her personality; fragile, yet durable, and beautiful.

Running past her reflection, she saw another in which made her run faster. She had almost made it down the hall in which extended further than a mother's love, until she glanced beside herself and saw nothing.

She stopped to catch a break and spun around aimlessly, attempting to find his face, a face, someone, anyone.

"Please come back." She said, panting. "Come back." She said again, forcing a tone filled with pleasure and modesty.

"You said that you were here for me... please come back."

Every hall echoed pure silence in return. She fell to her knees, in tears- feeling quite ridiculous.

"Why won't you come back to me?" She murmured in a tone of a child speaking back to their mother.

Footsteps away from her, a door soon opened, swiftly. She looked up as though she were lost in the park of a million children.

"I will never leave your side. My darling, you are a ray of sunshine lost in the darkness. Will you let me have you?" He said as he used the glass to reveal himself to her.

He was nearly as tall as the door, his skin resembled the sweetest piece of chocolate she had ever tasted,

and his hair fell like rain beside him;
He was a goddess.

Quite unsure of what she saw, she lifted her head up even further, got up and moved closer to that door. She faced him with the intent of hiding any fear, but she possessed none, only curiosity.

His lips were full, and they complimented the very well-crafted face that she saw before her.

She reached her hand out to touch him, she felt nothing but a questionable sensation. She tried again, failing to grasp his skin in which she presumed to be perfect.

She looked at him as he witnessed her efforts. His head fell, and his eyes met hers. Her perfectly blue, cloud-like eyes gazed into his with confusion.

"I am sorry, for I cannot measure up to be... more than this. I have watched you for years. I saw the anguish your life has given you. I asked to be released from the kingdom to provide you happiness... to give you true love."

"But how will you love me? How will you touch me? How will you hold me? You said that you were to make me feel warmth? How, when your flesh is nonexistent?

Your skin will never touch mine. I don't understand this. You are not real. How could I have fallen for a... what are you? A ghost? How could I have resorted to such desperate measures? You have to- "

"Don't tell me to leave. Please don't tell me to leave... because then, I would have to. You felt me touch you in your bedroom. I touched your back, I touched your spine, I-

"I cannot, I WILL NOT- she yelled.

He disappeared from the door's frame and brushed her from behind. He lightly grazed her hair again. She closed her eyes as he admired her aged skin, cover girl face, and perfectly blonde hair.

He pushed her body against his and kissed her neck, her cheek, her forehead, and then her precious lips.

He held her head in the palm of his hand as she opened her eyes. She investigated his opening doors as if they were the moonlight and motioned for him to kiss her once more.

She went to grab him, but she felt nothing.

She went to touch his hair, she felt not a strand.

She pulled away from him and readjusted herself embarrassingly.

She then walked backwards in a silent rage, and she looked at him and asked him, "What am I to do now that I can't have you?"

WHERE THERE

IS LOVE,

THERE IS

ROBBERY

"Ahhhhh, OH MY GOD who's there?!" Diana screamed as she ran to hide behind her kitchen counter after hearing a strange noise. She went to reach for a light and heard some scuffling at her front door. Where there WAS light, there was no more; it was pitch black. Now, all she could do was kneel and hope that she was just panicking for no reason because this was definitely not a dream.

As she stayed low, she saw a dark figure walk across her living room area. Dressed in all black, it was the reaper himself- there to take her life and anything else he desired. She held her breath, trying not to exhale-

but she did and when she did, he came

for her. She ran from side to side,

hoping to lose him but he met her face

only seconds later.

"Please don't- she blurted out,

but it was too late. He snatched her by

her neck and pulled her into the open

space. She yanked away from him as

best as she could, but he was too big.

He threw her over his shoulder and

stood in the middle of her living area.

She wondered if he even knew what

he was doing.

"Put me down and let me GO!"

"I'm going to put you down. When I put you down, I need you to be quiet... it will only take a minute." He said with confidence. He placed her down and backed away to watch her next move. In attempt to identify him, she looked up, but the darkness submitted zero justice. Sitting there, she realized that he was still watching her. She wanted to keep quiet until she saw him reach for his jacket.

He slowly removed his jacket and neatly placed it on the arm of her chair. He then stared at her again, reassuring her not to move with a look of intimidation- as if he were a father telling his baby girl "NO".

She inhaled, deeply. He took off his black shirt, before he could even get his arm out, she raised herself from the chair, prepared to run but she didn't. He placed his shirt on top of his jacket and stood in the same spot, awaiting some sort of signal. She analyzed him from head to toe.

From what she could see, the light that pierced her balcony window landed on the cuts in his abs and shoulders; she was weirdly intrigued. She lived alone for quite some time now, so she assumed that she was just thinking crazy, I mean for crying out loud, he was preparing to kill her.

He walked toward her and stood with his chest to her face. His large hands rubbed the top of her head in the roughest way possible. She tried her best not to scream. She grabbed his hand and tried to get up from the sofa. He slammed her back down and used both of his hands to hold her neck.

"Please!" She cried as tears chased the crevices of her chest.

"I don't talk much; I'd appreciate it if you didn't beg." He said in the slowest, cockiest way.

"But I, I can't die, please don't kill me, I'll do anything."

"You can't do anything for me that I can't take for myself."

Her eyes began to wonder crazily.

"You can't take love." she uttered in her mind.

"Please... I.. I-

He yanked her to her feet by her neck and pulled her to the kitchen. She tried to cooperate enough not to further piss him off, but persistence is often what got her in trouble.

"What's your name" she asked.

He didn't answer.

"WHAT IS YOUR NAME?!"

Still no answer.

"What is your name?! You're going to rape me? Kill me? Steal everything worth anything that I worked so hard for? The least you can do is tell me your name!"

He pushed her up against the marble countertop and held her still with his forearm against her throat.

"I told you to stop talking."

He began to open drawers until he found a knife worth using. He grabbed it and slid the tip of it across her face, then down around her collarbone, across her chest, and lastly, he laid it against her, as if imprinting a remembrance of this night on her skin.

"I am not a rapist; I do not wish to hurt you in that way. I will take the things that I need but I can't leave you alive... you are a potential problem, a liability. I do apologize but this just comes with what I do. You understand that, don't you?"

"But I wo-

"Shhh" he said in a soothing tone.

He took the knife and pulled her in front of him; positioning her well enough to slit her throat just right.

WHAT IS YOUR NAME?! she yelled out in fear of this question being her last. Tears ran from her eyes like husbands to their mistresses, quickly and desperately.

He raised the knife from the left side of her neck and whispered into her ear, "My name is Kevin."

Seconds away from the knife piercing her throat, she yelled "You can't take love, Kevin! Kevin, you can't take love!"

"SHUT UP!" He snapped in a baffling tone. He hadn't heard this plea before.

"But I'll love you, you can have all that you want, all that you need, but WITH ME!... Kevin."

He dropped his hand, turned her around, and looked her in the eyes. They stood in fatal silence for several seconds.

"I suppose you're right." He placed the knife on the counter and looked at her as if she were crazy. He wondered if she was just messing with his head.

She took a deep breath and decided to make the first move. She mounted him and began to kiss him all over. From there, they had each other all night.

Of course, she wondered how all this would really play out, but for now, she was safe, she was alive, she was okay, and Kevin was finally free.

MY NAME IS

KIM

It wasn't until July 21, 2014, that I experienced an unexplainable emptiness form from within my existence.

One could refer to it as sadness, a broken heart, or maybe even a baffled soul, but this, this was much different and far from the average assumption that anyone's mind could ever conjure up.

Don't get me wrong, I lost someone very significant to me- so I was definitely sad, I was definitely heart broken, and I was definitely confused. But as time pressed on, I became something else.

As time pressed on, I became someone else. Reflecting back, back, back to when things were different. I remembered what it was like for her to smile, for her to laugh, and for her to cry; I remembered what it was like for her to be alive.

Nothing would've made me happier than to wake up and it all just be this crazy, unbelievable, dream.

Nothing would've made me happier, but life, life shot me dead in between the eyes. The lips of reality yelled into my ears and into my face that my happiness did not matter-because she was gone, and she was never coming back.

No matter how long I stood there holding my mother's hand, hoping and praying that she'd simply open her eyes, it didn't matter because she was lifeless; completely gone and from that moment forward, I'd never get to hold her hand again.

I went to sleep after crying, as I did on many nights but this time, I felt weird. My heart was pumping extremely hard and there was this coldness releasing into my veins. I ran to the mirror, afraid of what I would see, but after catching my breath, I saw that I was okay. I looked like myself, therefore, I carried on with the day.

I had recently moved to a new area, it was nice, but it was so far away from all that I knew. My partner and I love to shop, so we were out, cruising the streets. We discussed this graveyard a few blocks away- every time we drove by it, time stood still.

On this day, we kept driving. The wind blew effortlessly across my face as I stared into the graveyard, wondering who could've possibly been staring back at me.

I became sad. I became angry. I became confused. I wanted to know where she was, and what the world had done to her; what God had done with her, my mother.

I needed her; she was my best friend, the life of my party, my alter ego, and my biggest fan. I became sad. I became angry. All over again.

When my mother passed away, I wished for her to have a gravesite that I could visit but we couldn't afford it. Unfortunately, she had to be cremated, which ruined me... it ruined me to know that she was burned. I couldn't help but be drawn to run through any graveyard, so that I might feel her presence somewhere, anywhere.

The day turned to night and there I was, unable to sleep again. Tears began to flow as I remembered the night that she left me.

The Dr. was so mean, he was casually texting with no eye contact as he relayed to us our mother's condition. He tried to encourage me to sign a DNR (DO NOT RESUSCITATE) form, but I declined after contacting my mother's best friend for clarity. He was truly pissed that I declined- stated that he'd never do his mother that way. Wow. still sinks my soul to the depths of me as I recount that moment.

I informed him that I was 1 of 9 of her children and to bring her back by any means... because who was I to take my mother away from them. Hours later... she slipped away from us all.

He was so cocky when he pronounced her dead, like he just KNEW that he was right, but she had already been gone, he lied to us; he was such a shitty ass individual. If my mother were here, she'd get him for hurting me.

I then thought about the pain that I carried after all of this. I became sad. I became angry.

My mother would have shown him what it meant to toy with her children.

I tossed, turned, rolled over, and then sat straight up as I held my head. I reflected on being fired from my job because I chose to fight for respect as a woman in a same-sex relationship. If my mother were here, she'd kill them for what they'd done to me.

I got up and left the house. I began to walk. *Where was my mother?* I was looking for her. I walked and then I slowed down as I approached the graveyard that we passed earlier.   It was big, it had so many people, I wanted to walk in. I had to walk in. I needed to walk in.

"Sometimes I just want to walk through a graveyard to feel her presence." I uttered these words some time ago. I was going to look for it. Her presence. I took steps closer and as I got closer, I became sad. I became angry.

It began to rain, the mud became very slippery, and so did my feet. I can't believe I wore these fucking shoes. I slid into a tombstone- I hit my head pretty hard. I looked up for light, I found some, but it was moving, toward me; the light was moving toward me.

I sat there for a moment and then I began to scoot backwards until I heard her voice. "Brittiny." I slapped the ground and shook my head. "Brittiny." I shook my head again with my eyes closed. I opened them and there she was.

"Kim!" I screamed. She smiled and said, "Let's get em!"

I asked her, "What are you talking about?" she replied, "Everyone that has ever hurt you since I've left; your soul called out to me."

"But where have you been? If you could've always come back, then why didn't you?" I cried.

"You wouldn't let me go. I was told that I could become part of you, so that you will never have to lose me again." She exclaimed in the most compassionate tone.

Kim stepped forward as if attempting to walk through Brittiny. She laid herself into Brittiny's body.

Brittiny screamed louder than a toddler as she curled herself into fetal position.

Her mother was very powerful but why? She looked so sweet, so beautiful. Why was this happening?

Brittiny woke up mysteriously in bed and well rested. The room was dark as she had always liked for it to be, but it seemed a bit darker today. She went into the bathroom and looked at herself, she looked even more like her mother than before. She began to remember her slip and fall at the graveyard and seeing her mom, Kim.

She questioned herself with no true clarity. One moment she was sure of what had happened, and the next, she deemed it all to be a sad dream.

She didn't know that her mother was waiting for the right moment to show herself. She had no idea what was coming.

Brittiny smiled and stroked her hair as if she were untouchable. Little did she know, she truly was.

SHE HAD A

DREAM

The lights were beaming into her face, shinning bright like the sun. Melanie had just stepped onto the stage to do what she loved most, sing. As her mouth began to open, she gazed over the audience looking for that one special soul to touch tonight.

She began to waltz across the stage, displaying the train on her gown, it was made of lace and extended further than the path that led slaves to freedom. She sang sensual tunes.

"I remember when you said, you wanna dance, and be my play toy.

Well baby I am Melanie, come over here boy."

She graced the stage like an angel; her voice and her presence were so damn beautiful. She walked closer toward her audience and reached her hand out to a man sitting next to a woman, presumably his mother, and she signaled for him to come up to the stage.

"Don't be scared to touch on me. I promise, I won't bite. I'm gone love you for infinity, so come and dance with me tonight."

Melanie sang as she tamed him, wild and freely. He smiled bashfully and in disbelief. This was a routine she'd done for many performances, to boost her ego and entertain her fans.

She began to sway back and forth until her eyes met his, and she was in his arms. He melted like butter on the front porch at grand mama's house, in the country, on a Sunday morning, which provoked her to do more.

Melanie placed his hand on the fattest part of her behind and the other on her waist side. She grinded on him as the crowd began to lose it.

Pressing forward with her sexual entertainment, she noticed

that the woman stared at her more intensely than someone's mother would, but she kept going any way.

The music stopped. The lights dimmed. They took the opportunity to explore themselves in the darkness with nothing but the crowd and GOD himself there to watch.

Melanie spun inward and teased him by licking the side of his face, and then grabbed his hair as if he were a dog. He was so bashful, but his eyes never strayed from her.

The crowd cheered them on, watching her give this man the time of his life. His "mother" soon got up from her seat and began to make her way to the stage.

Melanie held her mic to his lips and asked him, "What's your name baby?" He responded, "Cadence."

Without recognizing this woman's approach, she spun outward and then into a knife. Fans began to scream and run from her concert. The guards were approaching but it was too late, Melanie was being gutted by Cadence's mother, apparently, she didn't appreciate the performance.

"Have you lost your fucking mind Mona?! It was JUST a show!! It was JUST A SHOW!!"

Melanie laid there, hand against her bleeding flesh, leg hanging off the side of the stage, quickly fading away.

Mona came for Cadence, waving her knife while he ran for Melanie's last breath, hoping that he could save her.

"I am your WIFE, and I am TIRED of you disrespecting me!"

Mona raised her knife above his head, just in time for the guards to snatch her.

Melanie's eyes widened to Mona's statement, as she assumed, Mona was Cadence's mother. She struggled to bring life from her body and used her last words to say, "I'm sorry."

"I'm so sick of women like you!" Mona yelled. "You all take our men right in front of us but today, you had your last hoorah! Bitch you HAD a dream!"

Melanie faded away while staring at the stage lights, the only love she ever got to pursue. Cadence sat there in a pool of blood and guilt. She was gone.

BRUISES OF A

LOVER'S FIST

In a relationship where her husband never slept, and her eyes never stopped crying. Brandi, the righteous do-gooder, decided that it was time to strike back, but she worried about the bond that she created with God. How could she be a Christian woman seeking revenge on someone she loves, someone who was supposed to love her?

Sebastian, Brandi's beloved drug dealing husband, raped her ten-year-old daughter. He even shot Brandi up with Heroin, just so that she could be numb enough to watch him ruin her baby's body, her innocence.

How could she not want to make him pay? After all, she had lost contact with her family and her friends because she chose to stay with him for the betterment of their marriage, as well as her belief in forgiveness.

Everyone casted her out of their lives, everyone except her BEST friend. Kara was the greatest, she was there for Brandi when she was raped at their first outing to a house party; this is actually how she got pregnant with her daughter, Harmony.

Rape brought Harmony into this world and rape took her out, Brandi couldn't allow this to stand.

Kara even helped with naming Harmony because Brandi struggled with aborting her at first, due to the trauma of how she came about; drunken lust, sin, and being taken advantage of.

Brandi was a good girl. When he said that he wanted to go somewhere quietly to talk, she thought that he was just an intellectual guy who was truly trying to get to know her.

Her best friend was there for it all, and she convinced her that this blend of bad brought her some good, a blessing most would say, so Harmony it was.

As you can see, her best friend stuck around through it all and although Brandi vowed to never date again, Sebastian fought for her to change her mind.

They were great in the beginning, very typical happiness. He was a doctor, but he was also the biggest thug there was, and he made that very clear with all of the different types of friends he had.

Kara knew how deeply invested in the Lord Brandi was, which is why she supported her not leaving her husband after he murdered her daughter.

When Sebastian raped Harmony, he caused some internal bleeding that wouldn't stop, so baby girl drifted into the tomb of her mother's heart.

Kara was there for it all; she was the greatest best friend. I guess this was why she had been fucking Sebastian all along, right?

Sebastian was wanted by all women. The nurses did far more than ASSIST him, and the operating table was used for far more than surgeries!

Sebastian had a rude awakening coming. What would he do? What was Brandi going to do? Was she going to believe that GOD had a plan, or will she create one of her own?

Brandi tried to "roll with the big dogs," but her stunt got her beaten to death by Sebastian. On a chilling Halloween night, she created her own climax.

Little did he know; her ghost was coming back to haunt him and every woman that knew he was married!

Sebastian's in for a ride that he
will never be able to escape.

FAREWELL

This collection solidifies my passion and craft as an Author. I have enjoyed writing all my life, but each piece here has helped me to better acknowledge that this is what I was created to do.

I was meant to share stories. I was meant to inspire, empower, and connect; I was created to connect.

I'm bold enough to bare my lies AND my truths; that's what I love most about being an Author.

What I also love is that I can dress life up the way that I want, and I never have to wonder if I'm ever good enough, because somewhere all around the world, readers believe that I am.

I thank you for diving into the depths of me once more. Stay tuned.

ABOUT THE AUTHOR

"She's got something to say."

Brittiny D. Morehead- Author of The Naked Truth, I am Porcelain, and The Art of Words, was born August 3, 1991, in Fort Worth, Texas. Brittiny discovered the magic behind words very early in her childhood- where lots of sadness, drunken rage, and arguing took place. She couldn't fathom the reality of being in a family that seemed to be so dysfunctional; writing carried her away from it all.

Brittiny was a fatherless child who grew up with 8 of 11 siblings. Surrounded by so many kids, she wanted something of her own- someone even; so, she chose to accommodate her desires for attention by learning the art of sex. She became infatuated with boys because they made her feel that she mattered.

With boys came sex, with sex came love, and with love came rape, a miscarriage,

STDs, and growing up entirely too fast-
but through it all there was writing, and
there was poetry.

Brittiny attended Eastern Hills High
School, where she became President of a
well-known organization that worked
with distressed and disruptive teenagers;
UMOJA. She won a poetry competition
associated with this program and was
inspired to continue to utilize her voice.

Brittiny was thankful that she could heal
from and overcome her experiences, but
she couldn't quite let them all go- so she
launched her first poetic novel, The
Naked Truth, in July of 2014; where she

also experienced the loss of her mother only 10 days later.

Brittiny realized that she was nothing without the passion behind her words, so while grieving, she used the pain and tears as fuel to add to the fire that already burned inside her.

The Naked Truth, described to be "Maya Angelou meets Zane," sold out in less than two hours at its first book signing, located at a local Walmart.

Brittiny utilized that win to create more wins for her and aspiring writers- she launched her publishing company, Eat My Lyrics- a place where you're required

to devour every concept. She publishes
original content from individuals who
wish to elevate themselves. She also
mentors them into becoming better
creators.

Brittiny is a Spoken Word Artist, Public
Speaker, Ghostwriter, and Article Writer.
She continues to write so that she may
uplift, empower, and inspire people all
around the world.

Brittiny advocates for the voices that are
too afraid to speak, and she
acknowledges that she can articulate the
meaning of the power behind words.

For updates on the launching of each

title, please visit:

https://brittinydmorehead.com

LET'S GET CONNECTED:

STAY SOCIAL

<u>*FACEBOOK:*</u>

Author Brittiny D. Morehead (ADD ME)

<u>*FACEBOOK LIKE PAGE:*</u>

Talk That Shit Britt (PLEASE LIKE)

<u>*TWITTER:*</u>

@TalkThatShit_B (FOLLOW ME)

<u>*INSTAGRAM:*</u>

@TalkThatShitBritt (FOLLOW ME)

<u>*LINKEDIN:*</u>

Brittiny D. Morehead (CONNECT)

<u>*YOUTUBE CHANNEL:*</u>

http://www.youtube.com/c/TalkThatShitBritt (SUBSCRIBE)